Somewhere on the Edge of Words

by
D.M. Kraft

PublishAmerica
Baltimore

First printing

ISBN: 1-4137-2503-1
PUBLISHED BY PUBLISHAMERICA, LLLP
www.publishamerica.com
Baltimore

Printed in the United States of America

Dedication

This book is dedicated to the memory of my bestefar, a master carpenter and Freemason who served as the inspiration for "Winter Skeletons," but will always live in my heart as the Viking I first knew him to be; and of my bestemor, a woman who was as strong-willed and outspoken as her Norse ancestors, and had an infinite capacity for love.

Acknowledgements

Special thanks to Michael, my husband and best friend, for his extraordinary patience and the inner strength that constantly helps me to find my own; to Naomi, Sharyl and Darrell, whose parents, Bob and Alice, inspired the poems "Say When" and "To a Friend Lost Too Soon"; to Trish and Sandi, true friends and confidants; to Jari, Kay, Becky, Ravital and Leanne, who, with Trish and Sandi, opened my eyes to a world I only thought I'd known before, and who buoyed me through a mid-life crisis made even more horrific by the events of 9/11; to my mother, Inger-Marie, who was my first and favorite sounding board for the poems of my youth; and to the rest of my family - my father Eric, my god-parents Jerry and Dovis, and especially my sisters Anita and Kari - for always being there, no matter what.

And it is with particular admiration and gratitude that I also acknowledge my nephews, in service to their country during these confusing and chaotic times: Steven, who with the United States Marine Corps was among the first troops to respond in Afghanistan immediately following the 9/11 attacks; and Kris, soon to receive his commission with the United States Air Force.

Introduction

Two classic lines of poetry that always stand out in my mind are Emily Dickinson's "I heard a fly buzz when I died," and Dylan Thomas's "rage, rage against the dying of the light!"

Why these two lines? I suppose my obsession with that eternal quest for the meaning of life inevitably draws me to thoughts of death. It is a fact of life, and I don't fear it. Yet when death takes me I want to go with the knowledge that my existence had served a purpose.

I want my life to have meaning. I want to have a reason for being here, to find value beyond merely *being*. And so I constantly contemplate. And I search. And I wonder. It is a journey of the mind, one that takes me through a shadowed maze filled with as many gardens as false turns and dead-ends.

There is no map to show me where I need to go, but I do have one to remind me where I have been. That map is my poetry. Every line helps to guide me, taking me one step closer to understanding - and hopefully, one day, "*somewhere between one line and the next, to define the mystery of the why of me.*"

I don't expect to find that definition until it's too late to share it, but in this publication I can share at least part of my journey with you. By sharing my own journey, perhaps in some small way I can help make your path easier to see.

Patience! A single word ... and still a tale all its own.

- D.M. Kraft

Contents

Somewhere on the Edge of Words

The Why of Me

Somewhere on the edge of words,
with obstacles above me and deep chasms below,
this is my perch,
where I rest as I wait
to tell the tales that have been told to me;
to find the words that have been planted deep within me
by an unseen hand that I know, and yet do not;
to give them the ink they deserve,
and with it the voice they long to know;
and perhaps someday,
somewhere between one line and the next,
to define the mystery
of the why of me.

Patience! I breathe.
A single word past my lips
and still a tale all its own.

A New Me is Forming

I have dwelt in silence
withholding thoughts to avoid complication
trepidation
indignation

Speaking words as they ought to be spoken
a token
of social awareness

I was not me

Deep in my heart an ember flared
as I prepared
to cast the world aflame
with my pitiful name

To prove I have a voice
and the choice
to be heard
even through the din of a million others

More

To be remembered
long after the ember
burns itself out

To shout
"I am!"
and watch the echoes fly
even as I lie
cradled in the earth

To prove my worth
To be more than a speck of dust
adrift in this great universe

I can hold my tongue no longer

The fire has grown stronger
and will not be contained
detained
restrained
by a yoke of discretion

The fates have chosen a different path for me

I was not born to simply *accept*

The time has come for me to **project**
these pent-up thoughts

To loose the words that yearn to be spoken
a token
now of primal awareness

To be that which fate has designed

I am resigned

To reach toward that vision
despite the derision
of those who can't understand
or who try to demand
something that just isn't me

Let this be your warning
A new me is forming

Words Tumbling

Words tumbling
fumbling
from my brain
they somehow sustain me
a lifeboat in rough seas
an antifreeze
for the strong Arctic wind
that too often blows in
to this world I've found
around me
this piece of reality
that threatens my dreams
with its schemes
and empty promises

Thoughts forming
storming
into life
weaving stories rife
with fantastic notions
adrift over oceans
of fire
cold flames that inspire
a tempting burn
for the yearning soul

This is my treason
in defiance of reason
I create
to negate
the dark tides

I Am

Capture my spirit
with whispers
soft shadows
caress my soul
make me whole
out of the pieces of dreams
small fragments joining to one
and I have begun
to breathe
and I am
I
AM!

Evolution

Blistering
molten screams
burst the seams
    of my security

searing

    to the bone
    to the roots

scorching

scouring
savage storms
twist into tempests
tearing away what remains
filling drains
with the pieces of my life
    my hope
    my heart

until all that was
is gone

I am raw

empty

exposed

a desert canyon
worn smooth by raging rivers

running dry
to thwart the lie
   of salvation

or creation

the mountain has crumbled

a valley is born

and
whispering
verdant dreams
begin to fill the seams
   of my identity

weaving

   through the bone
   through the roots

growing

flowing
flowering seeds
blossom like weeds
filling the holes
in my soul
reinventing my life
   my hope
   my heart

until all that is
is enough

Obstacles Above Me...

The Aftermath of 9/11

In the Silence of a Crowded Room

In the silence of a crowded room,
at the café down the stairs,
my work abandoned at my desk,
I joined my colleagues there
to find the truth behind the talk,
and watch events unfold
that never could have been believed
from what we'd just been told.

Yet there it was, both live, and real,
on a screen too large to lie:
a scene that left us cold with shock
and numbly asking *why?*

In the silence of a crowded room
we watched the towers fall,
crumbling, under plumes of smoke.
A dark and hollow wall
soon spread itself across this land,
from sea to shining sea,
shrouding us in fear and grief
for Lady Liberty.

Yet like a beacon through the blight
she bravely held her ground,
reminding us to see that we
will not be taken down.

In the silence of a crowded room,
I watched those gathered near,
and saw each bore a common wound,
each face, so like a mirror.

We stood united with our pain,
as we followed terror's trail.
United now we share the scars,
and, united,
we'll prevail.

It is the Mourning After
* 9/12/01

It is the mourning after,
And there is a stillness in the air,
An emptiness that has taken hold
And will not let go,
Shrouding us in sorrow,
In shock,
In fear.

One life may be rebuilt,
Reborn,
For every life taken;
Yet every life taken
Is taken for good,
Stolen from us,
Whisked out of our waiting arms
In a single moment of madness.

A chasm has opened beneath us,
A void of impossible depths.

It will not pull us in.

Today,
We stand uncertain -
But we do stand.
Our feet are firmly planted on the ground,
And our eyes already begin to look ahead.

Tomorrow,

The sun will rise,
And so will we.

My Undoing
Autumn, 2001

In the space between now and eternity,
Where I once looked to find my dreams,
A strange void has blossomed into being,
An emptiness with iron-forged seams,
Sealing out whole realms of possibility,
Sealing in my own lonely screams.

And deep within this dungeon of obscurity,
I fall victim to my own dark crime,
Crouching in a corner with my madness,
Crying to the echoes left behind.
Excuses build impenetrable mountains,
Excuses make them crumble, after time.

Treasures I once hoarded for my pleasure,
Memorials to my own small name,
Grow tainted with the touch of expectation,
As portraits fall to dust in tarnished frames,
Abandoned by proprietors of glory,
Abandoned by progenitors of fame.

And therein lies my own direct undoing.
A selfish act, with selflessness assumed,
Stands open and exposed by indignation.
The mask is pulled away, the corpse exhumed.
Forgive me now, and hope will touch tomorrow.
Forgive me not, and hope stands dull and doomed.

Everything Has Changed

Autumn, 2001

Everything has changed
   And yet,

Here I sit at the same computer,
   Sipping the same coffee.
My desk is adorned with the same flurry of paper
   It has always suffered under.
My clock ticks away the moments,
   As it always has,
      As I procrastinate,
         As I always have,
My mind being more prone to wander than to focus.

At the end of the day
I'll drive home following the same route,
   In the same car,
Making the usual stops -
   The grocery,
      The dry-cleaners,
         The pharmacy.

I'll make dinner and clean the kitchen
   In the usual fashion,
Sharing the stories of the day with my husband.

We'll settle down in the evening to watch our usual programs -
   A sitcom,
      A news magazine,
         A documentary;

Then close our eyes until we do it all again.

And yet

Everything has changed.
I have grown old.

I see now through my mother's eyes,
Wondering if our world will end tomorrow,
    Courtesy of Cuba.

I see now through my grandmother's eyes,
Wondering how the *war-to-end-all-wars* will end,
    And to what end it will finally bring us.

And I see my grandmother,
    And her grandmother,
        And all the grandmothers before her,
Watching through my eyes
    And wondering
        Where this end will lead,
Because they could not know,
Because the harsh times of their lives
    Were so different than this harsh time in mine,
Because fear had a face
But terror does not.

Everything has changed.

    And yet,

This is a good world,
    One my grandmothers nurtured;
        One they dreamed into being
With their stories of wonder.

And more,

This is a world *beyond* my grandmothers' dreams,
   Where terror has sparked brotherhood,
      Where devastation has killed passivity,
Awakening the sleeping giant,
   That rebellious soul that birthed a nation
      With an infectious ideal.

In this good world,
America stands for unity and diversity
   And it is not an irony.

Yes, this *is* a good world,
Grown rich from my grandmothers' strengths.

It is a world where I have a voice
   While theirs were silenced,
A world where I have the chance to achieve
   Whatever I choose to strive toward,
And the only obstacles in my path
Are the ones I choose to accept.

This is a world where I am counted
   For the work I do
      And not for the hours I spend
Sitting at my paper-strewn desk,
While my mind wanders in search of my own dreams,
Because I *can* dream,
Because my grandmothers have given me this gift.

And yet...

Sunday, October 14, 2001

I am sitting in the cafe at one of America's giant bookstores, sipping my coffee. It is a delicious, full-bodied African blend.

The paper lies unopened before me. Like most Americans, I've been overwhelmed lately by too much news. I'd rather try to find my own words, so I've pulled out a notebook and pen. Now here I sit, ready to write something profound and enlightening.

But the muses are quiet today - as they have been for the past four weeks. Four long, cruel, agonizing weeks. It seems I no longer have the power to summon them. If they come at all it is at their own whim. So as I sit here sipping my coffee, I let my pen fly aimlessly across the pages and I try hard to listen. The voice of the muses is there somewhere. If I can just focus....

There, off to my left, a machine whirs away as someone stands waiting for their cappuccino or latte or whatever it is they've ordered. To my distant right a string of cash registers click along, recording the latest sales.

I wonder, briefly, what books people are buying today. The latest murder mystery, perhaps? Another Anne Rice horror story? And I wonder how anyone can read such tales now, when the horrors of reality are even more ghastly, more cruel, more damned than anything in print.

Maybe they're buying the latest magazines, ready to fill their minds with yet more stories of heroes and devils. Or could it be they're buying books about inspiration, meditation, divination, as they seek to banish the devils and think only of the heroes....

The rattle of dishes on a table behind me draws me away from these curiosities. I focus instead on the soothing serenade from the speakers above, the yearning strains of Pavarotti, his voice so warm, so compassionate. I don't understand the words, but it doesn't matter. Still he calls out to me, to my muses, helping them to guide my pen.

Still I don't know what to write.

I look up, to the windows just beyond the next table over, and I see

30

that the rain has stopped. The day is starting to look a little brighter out there in the parking lot. A stray ray of sunlight has somehow found a foothold despite the thick carpet of clouds.

I know it is temporary. The light will fade again soon. That's just the kind of day it is. Gray. Bleak. The world outside is sodden, while I sit inside, dry.

I think for a moment how odd it feels not to cry. The tears have been such a constant. Yet now that the universe itself is crying, I am not.

Instead, here I sit in a giant American bookstore, listening to an Italian tenor, sipping an African coffee, glancing at headlines about Afghanistan and trying to find the words my soul yearns to say but cannot, words the muses simply will not release. Not yet.

On the Loss of My Muse

Adrift without the glittering eyes of the night,
I seek the Voice.
I remember its cool embrace,
the tingling in my soul,
and I long for the reunion.

I'm tired of the heat,
of the warmth of endless days,
binding my eyes to Reality,
blinding them to the Shadows
that linger on the fringes of Truth,
burning out the Darkness where Dreams reside,
where Magic stirs Passion,
and Hope is conceived
Aborting it to Fact -

On the arid sands of Sanity I am a stone,
weighted to the earth,
without the chance to Fly.

Courage

I stumble out of wakefulness
drenched in the ether of the night
wanting nothing but the stillness
embracing that fragile forgetfulness
as though it were a cloak

I am a child under covers
protected from monsters

It is a lie
a dream out of sanity
marred by the mists that brush my skin
and seep into my pores
anesthetizing reason

It is time to let my feet touch the floor
a target for the claws that scrape the bed frame
and lift my face into the cooling sun

I can do no less
than to pry that quiet peace out of my numbing hands
and send it back into the river where it belongs
swirling through currents of ice
tauntingly out of reach

Anger Spreads

Anger spreads

a fungus taking root
in the dark
cold and red
desert damp
it permeates the soul
soil
and mushrooms
out of control
blooming spores
bursting to life
strife
a trick of evolution

Hatred grows

a tree out of flotsam
its canopy
bent and old
black from mold
rotting
it has been
eaten to the core
and talk of war
feeds its endless hunger
to pull us under
its gnarled branches
pretending protection
as

Alarms blare

a siren's invitation
soliciting convergence
insurgence
her cacophony
a warning
and mushroom clouds
are forming
cold and red
desert damp
to permeate the soil
soul
out of control

Fear ignites

a flaming arrow locked
its target lost
in dragons' plight
flight
from pages torn
histories forgotten
remembered
surrendered
to Alice
who wonders still
if venom heals
what it doesn't kill

I Looked Out Over Crystal Trees

I looked out over crystal trees
Like diamonds in the sun
Standing tall
Or bent and burdened
They glistened
Every one

    And though I sought the warmth of spring
    To leave the frost behind
    I smiled at the mysteries
    That vision brought to mind

Then later in the evening
As I watched the evening news
Another sight
Of blood and battle
Shattered
My fragile muse

    Winter clings and I protest
    But cannot deny its worth
    Despite the way it steals sweet life
    Budding from the earth

War persists and I distress
Over other budding lives
Lying still
Or bent and broken
Husbands
Babies, wives

Soldiers, rogues and innocents
Together in the end
It matters not if rights are wronged
Or whether enemy or friend

So like a crystal forest
This fragile, human race
Standing tall
Or bent, and burdened
In hope
Or in disgrace

Still I'd rather hold the image
Of diamonds in the rough
And believe one day we'll prove
We're made of greater stuff

Deep Chasms Below

A Child of the Sixties
a copy was left at "The Wall" in Washington, DC, October, 2000

A child of the sixties,
I toddled about on wobbly legs
as the world stumbled
and a president died.

And they all cried,
all those people on the news,
and in the *Life* magazine that lay untouched on the coffee table.

I touched it.

I ran my hand along the cover,
my chubby, baby fingers examining a widow's black veil,
a flag-covered casket.

Without knowing what, or why, or how,
still a nation's tears came down as rain upon my soul,
drenching me to the very core.

Then there was war.

An old war. A cold war,
though they said the jungles were hot
and deadly.

And our boys died.

American boys died.

I looked to the neighbor boys,
there in our cozy little corner of cookie-cutter suburbia,

and wondered if they, too, would die
somewhere in a hot, green jungle,
in a green and red Technicolor jungle
like the ones I saw at night on Daddy's Zenith,

jungles as distant as the little cabin up north
that took an eternity to drive to,
where I could hear the bombs go off at night
as our boys learned how to fight,
playing games at Camp Grayling -

games, like the neighbor boys in the park…
But I knew it was real,
as real as the musty sheets Mommy set under my chin,
when she tucked me in,
to protect me
from the distant thunder that was not thunder,
and boomed its way into my dreams,
reminding me to pray,
as I did every day,
for our American boys.

A child of the sixties,
still tasting the salt of my country's drying tears,
I was confused by the anger
that festered on the evening news.

So many different views,
when all that really mattered,
all that should matter,

was our boys;

our American boys.

A child of the sixties,
I saw my nation stumble,
but all I could do was hold out my hand,
my small, fragile hand,
and hope it might be enough,
to guide someone home.

I Weep in the Dark

I weep in the dark,
Alone,
Where even I am blind to the tears,
Dry, desert tears
That nourish nothing.

I weep in the dark,
In a small, closed room,
In a lonely place,
Where even I do not wholly go.

A Ripening Dawn

Wandering through dark fields,
in the grip of a deepening night,
I dream of that other place,
the one where grass is green and
meadows bloom in every color imaginable,
where shadows fall across my breast
and not within it,
where morning glows in warming shades of gold
and robins sing those cheerful melodies
that so used to revive me,
refresh me,
make me feel alive and good.

I wake to mourning doves instead.
Echoing my sorrow with their solemn cries,
they voice what I cannot
and fill my empty soul with yearnings I had forgotten,
helping me to remember the dream
and to grieve for it all the more.
Yet somehow, somewhere in the whispering trees,
the trill of a blackbird gives me solace,
and a new dream is kindled
out of the hope
of a ripening dawn.

Winter Skeletons

Tired eyes alight on brittle branches -
a cold reflection of a common fate:
winter skeletons alike on desert plains,
longing for indifference.

In the quiet of this frozen waste
are locked the lonely echoes of the lost -
and yet
too lonely to be lost,
too chained to be adrift.
Like empty dreams that scratch the shattered panes,
to unleash forgotten truths.

Tired ears awaken in the stillness -
a symphony of fragile chimes:
icicles against an angry wind
that strips the branches bare.

Harsh Winter

You sat beside me
As the wind howled
And the sky wept,
And we wept.
The night grew darker
The wind, colder.
Your eyes were mirrors of my own.

And we touched.

This morning,
The sun rose;
But my eyes still see darkness.

Forgive me -
I cannot forget.

Where I Rest As I Wait

Tomorrow Brings a Promise

Tomorrow brings a promise
    A whisper
        A dream
Born of every seed we sow today

But however much we nurture
    And harvest
        And reap
Some will fade and die, anyway

Others will just disappear
    A reward
        A prize
To a child with adventure in his soul

Or to someone filled with darkness
    With evil
        With lies
Who seeks a kind of malevolent control

However much we struggle
    We toil
        We fight
There is only one sure way to win

We have to choose with wisdom
    With instinct
        With heart
And find a way to plant the crop again

Scattered Thoughts

scattered thoughts
like leaves

    kidnapped by the wind
        taken at knifepoint

    severed

from headlines
    and deadlines
        and data unmined

           drifting

    without truth
without reason

    across and
      t
        h
          r
            o
              u
                g
                h
                and   b e y o n d

sometimes alighting
briefly
infrequently

    then taken again
        captured by indifference

            dreaming

    of fear
of conscience

    p u l l e d and pushed and t^{w}i^{s}t^{e}d

out of time

searching for anchors
           trussed into wings

In Dreams

In dreams the darkness falls away
To bright awareness, vivid day,
And everything's within my grasp -
I have just to reach or ask.
Great worlds of possibility
Open up and call to me.
In dreams.

In dreams the universe is mine,
Its treasures just for me to find.
Glory, honor, love, respect,
Await me there in high effect.
Through wisdom, truth and fair regard,
I've earned my place amongst the stars.
In dreams.

Yet no dream has a secret door
Through which a chosen few explore.
They're everywhere, for all to know -
To help us learn; to help us grow.
We need only look inside,
To grasp the power found astride
Our dreams.

Come morning we must all awake,
Our nightly visions, we'll forsake;
The vivid lines diffuse and die
'Til we can scarcely wonder why
We ever thought one moment more
Might be enough to learn the lore
Of dreams.

And yet a tiny spark remains
For those of us who hear the strains,
The melodies within our souls
That build our hope and feed our goals.
Please kindle well that quiet flame,
And never let the morning tame
Your dreams.

The Midnight Sun

I feel the sparkle of the midnight moon
And breathe the silence of its empty rays;
I hear its lullaby - the dreamer's tune -
And know the presence of more distant days;
I seek your love in every midnight moon.
I touch your lips in all my midnight dreams;
Then, waking as they scatter into ruin,
I smile at the sunlight's pleasant beams.
Anticipation guides me out of bed
And carries me into your waiting arms,
The pleasure of a love forever fed
By sunlit dreams and midnight's secret charms.

Yet now, my love, let's catch the midnight sun;
Our love shall grow beyond the darkest one.

To Tell
the Tales

Faith Long Forgotten

In the darkness he came, like a fierce angry wind,
With torrents of rain spewing evil and sin.
With thunder he raged, with lightening he preened,
As he searched through the night for souls to strip clean.

They followed his call, the lost and confused,
Prepared to be victims, to be thrashed and abused.
Their neglected cries through tormented years
Had embittered their spirits and clouded their tears.

Hate was the answer to questions not asked.
Faith long forgotten, the die had been cast.
Their souls filled with anguish, their hearts filled with pain,
They followed a master who promised them fame.

They walked through the night, they slithered, they crawled,
To pledge their cold lives to the master who called.
Forgetting the promises made long ago,
They followed a pathway where hope need not grow.

Anguish and torment and pain for all time,
Made them secure, and unaware of the crime.

I Walk Ancient Roads

I walk ancient roads
Reading codes
Meant for other eyes;
Words drawn from distant skies
Left to crumble in the dust...

    Left to crumble, not to die -
    For somehow I
    Would stumble on the truth,
    The harsh lessons of my youth
    Lending strength to weary hope...

Lending strength to help me cope.

There is so much to learn,
Even while I burn
With unspent fury.

    So much lost
    To pay the cost
    Of love remembered,
    Of love surrendered

To keep me bound
To ancient roads,
Reading codes
Meant for other eyes;
Words drawn from distant skies,

Left to crumble in the dust…

Left to crumble in my hands,
Through scattered sands
Where wisdom hides away.
Even time might not betray
The knowledge hidden there,

The knowledge that my dreams have shown.

There is more to life than here,
More than what is clear
To shielded eyes.

So I search;
And it is worth
The lives remembered.
The time surrendered

Shows me why
I walk ancient roads
Reading codes
Meant for other eyes;
Words drawn from distant skies,
Left to crumble in the dust.

Dreaming

Dreaming, in that way I do,
I melt into the mist,
Where edges fade, and darkness too,
And I need not resist.

My journeys there are safe and warm,
For I have full control
In that place where wild adventures form,
Amusement for the soul.

It takes me to the Amazon,
Or some new, exotic land
For a dangerous liaison,
With old foes there, close at hand.

It takes me into forests dark,
And deserts harsh and wide;
It shows me stars that fade and spark,
Then leads me deep inside

To find the damsel in distress,
Or the brave and noble knight,
Or perhaps the warrior at rest
From some preempted fight;

We might find a crumbling ruin,
Or perhaps an ancient tome,
Or the chords of some forgotten tune,
Meant to guide ancestors home.

Whatever lies in wait for me,
In that netherworld of mind,

It gives me hope to wander free,
Through portals locked in time;

A trip into the wild west,
With a horse and holstered gun,
Like cowboys on some desperate quest
To find the land we've won.

Or a journey down the Nile,
Where the pyramids still shine,
Like the castles reaching skyward
Along the river Rhine.

The stories never cease to rise,
The heroes never die,
And I often find, to my surprise,
They sometimes even cry.

Dreaming, in that way I do,
I find a kind of peace.
Reality might be the glue,
But I prefer the crease,

Between what is and what can be,
And perhaps what never will,
That place where I can finally see,
What lies beyond each hill.

I have to take this time to dream,
Before tomorrow comes,
And challenges the things that seem
The fear of all our sums.

The Comedy of Stars

I wept under the moonlight,
beneath the brilliance of the galaxy.

The stars that brought life to the heavens,
only brought tears to my eyes.
Stretching into infinity,
they sparkled and twinkled
as though restlessly waking.

I sat in agony, restless
and begging for sleep.

Looking up through tear-clouded eyes,
I saw a star blazing a trail.
It flew a path across the sky,
then disappeared into the far realms of infinity.

I wished that all of the stars would follow
and darken the world,
hurling me into the blackness
my mind already knew.

I wept in loneliness and uncertainty,
yet marveled at the liveliness of the stars -
so brightly ecstatic and yearning for life.

I wept under the moonlight,
under the comedy created by the stars…

Or was I the comic,
for they laughed while I cried?

Angel Bird

As rainbows filled her tired eyes
she watched a bird with angel wings
soar into a crystal sky
and float beneath a cloud of rings.

    The cloud came down and opened wide,
    and took the little bird inside.

She was sad to lose her angel bird,
and wondered where the cloud might lead,
but then a distant voice she heard,
with questions asked of mortal greed.

    The voice was gentle, true and pure,
    but had not come to speak with her.

An answer came with quiet songs
that drifted like the summer wind -
a confession of a thousand wrongs
a whisper of a thousand sins.

    "No!" she cried. "That is untrue!"
    and yet, within her heart she knew.

"Oh, little bird, what chance have I
to pass beyond great heaven's door,
when you offer such a stark reply
and my own sins are so much more?"

    Her solemn cry could scarce be heard
    above the small, repentant bird.

And yet, the songs all ended now,
the great and wondrous voice returned,
with gentle words explaining how
the little bird would not be spurned.

 And then the joyous, little one
 rode angel wings beyond the sun.

Now the cloud came near to her
and swirled above her burning eyes,
to fill them up with heaven, pure,
a vision no one could despise.

 "Oh heaven, how I long for you!
 But, alas, my sins are true."

She wept for all that she had lost
throughout a life so dark and stained;
she wept to pay the bitter cost
for perfection never once attained.

 And then the voice came, loud and wise:
 "Come, shed your criminal disguise!"

"The time has come for you to see
beyond the mask of humankind.
What you are will set you free,
when what you were is left behind!"

 And then she blinked her vision clear,
 to find, beneath the cloud, a mirror.

Reflecting back, she found herself -
an image dark with fear and pain.
Hands that once had reached for wealth
now reached behind her in disdain.

Oh, what a hateful thing she saw!
Oh, mortal being, cold and raw!

But then another image came,
struggling through her crimson skin;
a brighter, whiter kind of flame
began to pull her darkness in.

As though she had been newly born,
her soul came forth to greet the morn.

She floated now beneath the cloud,
no longer weighted to the earth,
and felt her own songs, pure and loud,
heralding her second birth.

Oh, such a joyous thing to find
that hope remains for humankind!

The angel stood within the door
and reached a hand to take her own,
and led her to forevermore,
above the clouds where heaven shone.

The cloud came down and opened wide,
and took the little bird inside.

And then the joyous, little one,
rode angel wings beyond the sun!

The Ink They Deserve

Surround Me with a Garden

Surround me with a garden
A myriad of hues
Just like an artist's pallet
Full of vibrant reds and blues
A crimson rose, an iris
A daffodil and more -
One of every color
A visionary roar!
The music should be Mozart
And some Vivaldi, too
Playful, light and hopeful
To send the proper cue
The talk should be of legacies
What fruits my life has borne -
Enough, I hope, to fill the voids
Embraced by those who mourn.

To a Friend Lost Too Soon
For Alice

It had never occurred to me
we would have to say good-bye to you so soon.

Your kind heart,
your caring nature,
your high spirits,
your infectious laughter -
these I had thought to be as certain
as tomorrow's sunrise.

But tomorrow is just a promise;
and an indistinct one at that,
full of muted grays
and blurred lines.

Into that promise,
into the uncertainty it offers,
we try to provide the details.

We paint the images
we expect to find within that tomorrow,
the faces of those we love,
those we cannot imagine
any tomorrow to be without.

We paint them in bright colors,
using a full and rich pallet,
to show how they enrich our lives.

But the canvas is not ours alone to control.

Tomorrow comes before the paint can dry,
and the colors sometimes run together,
changing images we thought were unchangeable.

Changing them,
but not erasing them.

I still see you on that canvas.

I always will.

I see you in the playful reds,
in the vibrant and fiery oranges,
in the warm and soothing yellows,
in the joyful, brilliant whites.

The colors of your life have enriched my own,
and will remain a part of me
for all the tomorrows yet to come.

Say When
In memory of Robert

I remember the Fourth of July:
fireworks in the backyard,
A & W root beer, and
ping-pong in the garage.

You filled my mug and told me to say when.

I said "stop" and you kept pouring.

I said "stop"
again and again,
but soon the root beer spilled over the sides.

Finally I said "when,"
and finally you stopped.

I suppose in all things
we all have to know when
to say when.

But it's hard to say "when" to you today.

You've always been there:
a big man
with a big voice.

Your eyes were hard,
but your smile, warm.

I remember laughter...

I remember a motorcycle,
and airplanes,
and water-skis…

I remember a comedian
water-skiing up north
behind our boat -
you sat on a lawn chair and read the paper!

I remember a man
who knew how to have fun,
but who also knew when to say *when.*

Some joys gave way to others,
and life went on.

And now it's time for us to say when,
and to let our lives go on
without you.

It's time for us to let go.

It's time for you to reach ahead,
to find that special joy we all aspire to,
and to prepare the way for us to follow.

Robert, we love you…

When.

I Hurt When You Hurt

I hurt when you hurt and you hurt for me,
And on grows the cycle exponentially,
Feeding and growing and going to seed -
Until hurting grows hurtful with unrecognized greed.
You push and I push and shields are enforced.
Words become hateful - unspoken remorse
Fuels our anger and feeds on our pain,
And thus starts the cycle all over again -
Forgiveness not granted, nor asked as we seethe,
While guilt burns so deeply we can't even breathe...

When you hurt when I hurt and I hurt for you,
How can we remember, and hold to what's true?
I hope I can help you and you can help me
Acknowledge this cycle - allow it to be,
And turn its raw hunger, its malignant greed
Into something useful, a new kind of seed -
One that reminds us repetitively
That I hurt when you hurt and you hurt for me.

So Many Things I Need to Say

So many things I need to say
But the time is never right
So many games I start to play
Drawing shades against the light
It's always best to keep my heart at bay
To thwart the darkness of pure night
It doesn't matter, anyway
It's really pretty trite

'Cos even when I state my case
The words just come out wrong
All twisted up and out of place
Mixed with thoughts that don't belong
Like I'm winded, in a losing race
When I thought I'd started strong
Yet I never even found my pace -
Out of synch, all along

So please excuse my quiet thoughts
Somehow I'll work them through
It might appear, at times, that I am lost
And perhaps, at times, that's true
But our paths are intricately crossed
So when I find a turn that's new
I'll pay the toll, at any cost
That guides me back to you

This Busy World

This busy world in which we live
is persistently demanding.
It takes and takes and rarely gives:
our lives, it is commanding.

It fills my mind and chills my heart
'til I grow weak with anger.
Then icy words pull us apart
before we ever see the danger.

Perhaps a real apology
should never need repeating.
A spokesman for psychology
might say the words are cheating.

And transgressions made not once, but twice,
must void the words, "I'm sorry."
But even in this world of ice
that cannot end the story.

The careless wrong I do today
might come again tomorrow.
Chaos leads my mind away
'til I forget past sorrows.

Who I am unto myself
is an easy shield to wear;
but it keeps me from the joyous wealth
of life we're meant to share.

I must forget my selfishness -
it's such an empty greed,

for it can only end in loneliness
and lock my heart in need.

Together we must try to force
this insanity aside.
We must not seed the dark remorse
that haunts us deep inside.

We must push ourselves to see and hear
the truths hidden in the void,
before everything that we hold dear
is summarily destroyed.

To Define the Mystery

Questions

Questions
floating like whispers
quietly sifted
like sands tumbling
through my fingers
softly gliding
along the lines that define me
the marks that speak my name
then taken by the winds
a million tiny grains
called to other places
to other hands
cast away
unanswered

Until I follow

Above, the Sky

Above, the sky -
and what beyond?
I cannot help but wonder.
Could there be significance,
To this spell it puts me under?

We stand so tall upon this rock,
We build, create and dream;
And yet among those distant stars
We are but small and fragile beings.

All things will, one day, decay,
Great paintings fall to dust,
And poets words will be reclaimed
As languages adjust

To fit a new eternity,
A dawning, different age.
There will come a time for us
To turn that final page.

What then?
I ask those hungry stars
That taunt me with desires
To search beyond this universe
And squelch these raging fires.

They burn me through and through with fear,
For what we have will fade -
And, more than that,
will die complete,
These treasures that we've made.

And then no more…

…Perhaps.
Unless we are remembered -
Ah! That is what I wish for us
When this Earth must be surrendered!

To spread the seeds of humankind
Beyond the farthest star,
Revealing what we once had been,
And relearning what we are.

Today my eyes look heavenward,
Yet my heart is planted here,
And my dream is for humanity
To project what makes us dear.

Listen

Shh. Quiet. *Listen.*

Not just to the sounds in the air,
but to the soft murmurings it shelters.

A great exhalation,
the breath of the Earth,
whispers of memories our elders have yet to know,
speaks to us of futures that have been forgotten,
of dreams that have been spent,
of yesterdays yet to come.

The pulse of every heart that has beaten,
the cry of every babe ever born
is there in that breath.

Listen and they'll tell you:

This tiny speck of rock,
this pebble in the universe,
has an infinite spirit,
because of them,
because of us -
and in spite of us as well.

Shh. Listen.

Then join your voice to the song.

Tomorrow's Tomorrow

As the stars drift away from the cold, empty sky
And the sun wanders in like a luminous spy
Life comes out of the gray but refuses to form
As it waits for the dawn of a still newer morn

Caught between layers and lost out of time
Where gods are subverted and dust is sublime
Where villainy crumbles and victory fades
And no one is cheering for freedom parades

This is the space where tomorrow turns
Where decisions are weighed as humanity learns
That every step forward leaves something behind
And each yields more choices, and none are benign

The future seems vast as we gaze through the mist
Despite careless deeds, more options exist
Since tomorrow's tomorrow seems so far away
We've nothing to fear in the heart of today

Yet as the sun rises to show our next path
And we take that step knowing there's no turning back
We must reconsider the strength of our faith
In the wisdom that guides us, before it's too late

I Play

Beyond your watchful eye,

I play

with Crayola colors
blending
conception and confusion
into a kaleidoscope of illusions

and I forsake confession for delusions.

I ponder,

still I play

in a game with a tedious score,
and like some ephemeral whore
I long
yet fear
for more.

Sometimes I find a precarious victory.

Like in some fairy-tale history
I reach for the stars,

but they fade fast.
They cannot last.
Nothing can
without you.

And it is you I seek
even as I hide.

It is a game without aim;
a gain without pride.

Still
I play.

Patience!

Spiraling Through Time and Space

Spiraling through time and space
I sometimes feel so out of place
Like I'm not even keeping pace
With this thing they call the human race

Each lap reveals another page
Another book, another age
And no advice, however sage
Will freeze the moment, lock the cage

Thus one by one my visions fly
They merge into a whispered lie
That helps me when explaining why
I never had the time to try

Yet as the seconds tick away
Another hour, another day
I lose my focus, start to stray
And watch my dreams all fade to gray

My journey's had a tepid run
I stumble at each starting gun
Though sometimes it's been wild and fun
I've never lost, nor have I won

Perhaps I'll test the track once more
I'll walk one lap, just to explore
And then I won just run - I'll soar
Until I earn the chance to score

In the Garden of My Thoughts

In the garden of my thoughts,
Grow some incongruent things -
Deadwood and choking vines,
Join mushroom fairy rings;
Irises and roses,
Bloom through the dead of night;
Thorny burrs and poison oak,
Give a constant, hearty fight.

I never know from day to day
Just what my thoughts will find.
Sheer joy and laughter will
Melt to tears from time to time.
Deep fissures in the ground
Can draw me down with roots of steel,
Surrounding me with empty dreams
And daring me to feel.

Yet in the distance, far above,
A single bud will grow -
A burst of color through the gray,
A sign of hope, I know.
And as I watch, it starts to spread,
A rainbow starts to form;
And then the smiles come again,
As laughter ends the storm.

When asked which plants I'd alter;
What changes would I make?
"Not a one," would be my answer;
For why would I forsake
The highest of all highs,
Just to end the lowest of all lows?
One balances the other,
And they each help me to grow.

To Count the Sorrows

To count the sorrows of my life
is to count each drop of rain
in the torrents of spring,
while I, like the fragile leaf,
cling to hope by a slender thread
of possibility,
bending unmercifully in the deluge
that so seeks to break me,
to sever the thread
and send me thrashing through the winds -
until the Earth,
at last,
consumes me.

To count the joys
is to count a single ray of sunshine.
Too small to part the clouds,
barely strong enough to filter through,
still it warms my soul,
refreshing my spirit
enough to endure the storm.

The count of sorrows is the greater number.

But sorrows are feathers,
while joys are solid gold,
tipping the scales at every measure.

A single joy can bend clouds into rainbows;
just as a single smile can turn the tide of tears.

To count the sorrows of my life
is to waste precious time.

I choose, instead, to build rainbows.

Awakening

I am coming awake.
The sun grows within my eyes
as though newly born,
newly risen;
and the path before me has come alight
as it never had before.

I can finally see beyond the shadows,
and even they grow lighter.

The twigs and brambles
that have for so long sought to catch my feet
are falling to dust.

The fetid air
that has for so long sought to burn my eyes
and poison my lungs
has fallen victim to healing breezes
that blow past me and through me and in me -
so fresh, so clean, so sweet,
I revel in their touch.
And the riverbed
that has for so long been dry,
but for the scattered pools of bitter, stagnant water,
has once again begun to flow
with a bubbling rush of playful purity
And it beckons me to join the game.

Soon, perhaps.

But for now,
at least I can sit at its edge
and watch,
as I let it dance across my toes
and soothe my weary feet.